THE
TERRORIST PLOT

NOVELS BY HARRY KATZAN JR

The Mysterious Case of the Royal Baby

The Curious Case of the Royal Marriage

The Auspicious Case of the General and the Royal Family

A Case of Espionage

Shelter in Place

The Virus

The Pandemic

Life is Good

The Vaccine

A Tale of Discovery

The Terrorist Plot

THE TERRORIST PLOT

A MATT AND THE GENERAL ADVENTURE

A NOVEL

HARRY KATZAN JR.

THE TERRORIST PLOT
A MATT AND THE GENERAL ADVENTURE

iUniverse books may be ordered through booksellers or by contacting:

iUniverse
1663 Liberty Drive
Bloomington, IN 47403
www.iuniverse.com
844-349-9409

ISBN: 978-1-6632-2233-6 (sc)
ISBN: 978-1-6632-2234-3 (hc)
ISBN: 978-1-6632-2235-0 (e)

Library of Congress Control Number: 2021908722

Print information available on the last page.

iUniverse rev. date: 04/28/2021

For Margaret, as always

FOREWORD

*T*he last few years in the United States have been filled with confusion, excitement, and disappointment. The 911 events have changed almost everyone's concept of security, and we have learned exactly just whom we could trust and whom we couldn't. The manner with which the 911-crisis was handled taught us an important subject. Things happen about which we have no knowledge and no established methods of handling.

In short, here is the scenario. A team of middle-eastern men armed with box cutters hijacked four American airliners. Two of the airliners were crashed into the World Trade Center. One plane was crashed into the Pentagon. The fourth one was intended to crash into the White House, but brave passengers overpowered the infiltrators and crashed the plane into a field in Pennsylvania. Several thousand persons were killed, and there was much confusion on exactly how to proceed. The skies were cleared of aircraft, except for the President's Air Force One which made a fast ascent from Florida and flew in a westerly direction. Security around the capital was excellent and the situation was well controlled, even though the President had been at a grammar school talking to young students. The President eventually returned to the White House, and the crisis appeared to be under control.

The U.S. always does the right thing, and many middle-easterners were permitted to leave the country for their personal security

The attack on the United States might have been misguided, since some influential middle-easterners said it was a mistake to awaken a sleeping giant. We responded with power and determination.

The country initiated a global war on terror and strengthened its internal security. One issue that wasn't resolved was the question of who sponsored the 911-attack. Was it the attackers themselves, or was it a terrorist group that paid another organization to do the actual work? In the case of 911, it was a middle-eastern organization financed and led by a person named Osama bin Laden. After bin Laden was eliminated by the United States military, no one immediately stood up and took over the offensive.

Terrorism was reduced to small operations and on the recruitment of people for doing terrorist work in the middle-eastern countries and elsewhere. Influential television ads were and are constructed to convince young persons to adopt the cause of the Muslim party. Small well-financed terrorist operations are attempted using foreign and domestic people. In many cases, the terrorists themselves do not know the leaders and sponsors of their teams.

One of the major problems in defending against domestic terrorism is that the persons are young, well educated, and both male and female. They know U.S. customs, since many of them are U.S. citizens with valid passports, driver's licenses, and COVID-19 vaccination cards.

This book describes a terrorist plot in the United States that should be of interest to many readers.

The Author,
May 1, 2021

PROLOGUE

Matt Miller and Ashley Wilson met in Dr. Marguerite Purgoine's creative writing course, and frequently got together after class at Starbucks to discuss items of interest, as students commonly do. They were friends, because they liked each other. After completing their university studies, Matt became an established mathematician and a prize-winning golfer. Ashley was seeking celebratory status as an actress. Dr. Purgoine, known personally as Anna for some unknown reason, was a distinguished professor and award-winning author. Matt's grandfather, Les Miller, was a retired general in the U.S. Air Force, and subsequently the founder of an influential political polling company. He was referred to as "the General," because of his collection of major accomplishments. The General was wealthy and liked to help people. This led to several interesting adventures for Matt and the General, often involving Ashley and Anna.

Like most persons in the modern world, they were hit by the Pandemic of 2020 as the worst thing that has ever happened to them. Words like shelter in place, facial mask, social distance, and wash our hands for 20 seconds were commonplace and still are. Businesses, restaurants, bars, movie houses, sporting events were totally, if not partially, changed, and many people think our way of life in modern countries will never return.

COVID-19 is the name of the pandemic that took most people by surprise. History will say that it originated in China and spread from there to the rest of civilized society. The virus is highly contagious, and people were encouraged to maintain a social distance from other individuals when out in public and to stay indoors when possible.

Matt, the General, Ashley, and Anna were influential in searching for the source of the virus and evaluating the various theories that were generated by COVID-19's appearance on the face of the earth. Matt, the General, Ashley, and Anna, frequently known as the Team or The General's Team, worked very closely with government sources, and Ashley was awarded the National Medal of Freedom, the United States' highest award for achievement by civilians.

But, we're getting away from the story. Matt and the General were getting tired of the golf course at the Country Club and decided to give Hilton Head Island in South Carolina a try. They had heard that many foursomes drove straight down and got a couple of good rounds of golf and some nice dinners in a long weekend. Matt did the research and chose the Big Dune Hotel and Golf Course as the place to go. The hotel was exceedingly expensive, but a pick-up at the Hilton Head Airport was available and golf and dinners were included. Matt flew Little Man, the General's private plane, to Hilton Head and a promising weekend was in store. After checking in, Matt and the General went down to look at the golfing facilities and especially the course.

Something unexpected occurred. They ran into General Mark Clark, a four-star general, who had retired from the Army as Chairman of the Joint Chiefs of Staff. Our General and General Clark were former associates, but their relationship was professional and their interface was through the President of the United States. In the military, a general is an appointment for life.

General Clark was concerned about a crucial project that he had volunteered to undertake but he needed help to resolve. As the President stated it, we have intelligence concerning an attack by aircraft of a vulnerable target in the States. It was what the President had heard from the President's Daily Brief. After the country's success in eliminating Osama bin Laden, bin Laden's brother indicated he was obligated to respond with a terrorism attack of a significant magnitude on the United States. In a subsequent government intercept, it was determined that Hilton Head Island was to be the center of the operation. Surveillance determined a location, the person, the date, and a team of Iranians that engage in the attack. It was also indicated that the sophistication level of the planned operation was exceedingly high. The participants involved with the terrorist threat were permanent residents of the United States, and held U.S. passports, driver's licenses, university diplomas, and actual wives and children. They were transparent to the American authorities.

This is where the story begins.

CHARACTERS IN THE BOOK

The General – Les Miller. Former military General and Humanitarian. P-51 pilot and war hero. Has bachelors, masters, and doctorate degrees.

Matthew (Matt) Miller – Professor of Mathematics. Has PhD degree. Grandson of the General.

Ashley Wilson Miller – College friend of Matt Miller. Former Duchess of Bordeaux. Married to Matt Miller. Has Master's degree and is a Receiver of the National Medal of Freedom.

Allen Weinberg – Professor of Computer Science. Has PhD degree. Language specialist and is former associate of Matt and the General.

Marguerite Purgoine - Retired creative writing Professor and an associate of the team. Has PhD degree. Known as Anna for some unknown reason.

Sir Charles (Buzz) Bunday - Former P-51 pilot. Army buddy of Les Miller. Member of the British Security Service. Knight of the United Kingdom.

General Clark - Mark Clark. Former Four General and Chairman of the Joint Chiefs of Staff.

Harry Steevens – Expert mathematician and former college friend of Matt Miller. Policeman in Hilton Head.

Mary Brown – Policeman in Hilton Head and grammar school teacher.

Atalus – Terrorist leader.

Max Smith – electrical engineer.

Nancy Small – government statistician and math tutor.

Michael Clark - student of Matt Miller and grandson of General Mark Clark.

And Others

PART I
HILTON HEAD

1

THE GOLFERS
SPREAD THEIR
WINGS

It was a beautiful morning and Matt and the General were out on the Country Club golf course. The two golfers had just finished the ninth hole. Matt was always the first to start a conversation on just about any subject. Today, Matt was on the case of the condition of the golf course.

"Is this place getting shabby?" asked Matt. "The grass looks worn out like a crusty old carpet."

"You're just tired of it," said the General. "You know every dip and rough spot and don't have to think about them and also less on your golf techniques. You're just plain bored."

"I suppose you're right," said Matt. "Why don't we go somewhere else like the golf course in the Freehold, New Jersey area?"

"Here's your answer. Because the players are a bunch of rookies," replied the General. "To them, just to hit the ball is a big deal, and they contemplate the universe at every hole."

"Why don't we try South Carolina?" asked Matt. "One of my student's grandfather and grandmother live in Hilton Head, and they are supposed to have the best courses in the country. Maybe even the world."

"In the world," answered the general. "That's a pretty good reputation, and this is a big world. Do you believe it?"

"That's what the student said." said Matt. "He could be right."

"How do they get down there?" asked the General. "Most people work and can't exactly walk out the door, like we can."

"He says that four golfers climb into a Mercedes and drive non-stop from New Jersey to Hilton Head," said Matt. "Maybe they take Friday or Monday off, or both, and get in a couple of good rounds and some good dinners."

"We could fly down," said the General, "and rent a car."

"Maybe, the courses have a pick-up service and a couple of good restaurants, so a golfer doesn't have to leave the property," added Matt." Some of golfers and their families have a residence down there also. The student's name is Michael Clark, do you think he's related to someone we know?"

"There are thousands of Clarks in the country," answered the General. "Let's do it. We can go down Friday evening and return Sunday evening or Monday morning."

"You're on," said Matt. "Next weekend? It will be good to get out of here, if only for a couple of days."

Sounds good," said the General. "You find the course."

"I'll start with the student and then go to *Golfing Times*," answered Matt.

Both golfers were pleased and the rest of the current round on the C ountry Club course was pleasurable again.

Matt and the General had driven separately to the course, and the General drove straight home. Matt went to his office and called the General on his cell phone.

"We forgot something," said Matt. "We didn't think about our better halves. Ashley would love to go to down to Hilton Head, and I don't know about Anna.

"I thought about that also, but you are quicker on the draw," said the General. "I'm sure Anna wouldn't mind going also. What do you think they would do?"

"I'll look into it," replied Matt. "Our friend the Internet should be able to help us out. I'll call you back in a couple of hours. If you don't answer, I'll assume you are otherwise occupied.."

An hour later, Matt called the General again.

"Hi," said Matt. "There is more to this Hilton Head than just golf courses. There are many restaurants and good shopping. I would say excellent shopping. There is an upscale mall named Shelter Cove. It's a new outside mall."

"What's an outside mall?" asked the general.

"It's a collection of organized luxury shops. They have specialties and also ice cream and hamburger shops, and even an outlet for craft beer. Close to Hilton Head is a community named Bluffton, and it has an Outlet Center. Actually, there are two outlets, referred to Tanger One and Tanger Two. Tanger One is supposed to be better. The good golf courses are in Hilton Head and Bluffton. There is another community called Sun City but the magazine didn't say much about it. It says it is a gated community with three golf courses."

"Okay, why don't you choose a course with a hotel and some kind of transportation service?" said the General. "Then if the ladies say they are interested, we an go. You and Ashley have a schedule of classes, so you make the itinerary."

'"Okay," said Matt. "I'll do it."

Matt planned on shopping around as far as the lodging was concerned, but got a hit on his first try. It was nice to be flexible about the price. In fact, the more expensive, the better. Matt chose a new property with two golf courses and a fabulous restaurant, specializing in filet mignon and lobster. Its name is the Big Dune Hotel and Golf Courses with airport pickup and facilities for storing golf clubs between visits. Matt made a reservation for a two-bedroom suite for Friday, Saturday, and Sunday. They could fly down Friday afternoon and return Monday morning. Monday classes would have to be worked out. He would think of something.

2

THE HILTON HEAD ITINERARY

A shley was there when Matt got home.

"How was your golf?" asked Ashley.

"It wasn't that great," said Matt. "Neither of us played as well as usual. Maybe we need more practice."

"You guys go to the same course all the time," said Ashley. "You're tired of it. That's normal. You need a change."

"You know, that course is getting pretty shabby, and I think we are getting used to it," said Matt. "I think you are right. You are always right, Ashley."

"Of course," said Ashley. "I thought you knew that."

"As far as the course is concerned," said Matt, "that is what the General and I have been thinking about," said Matt. "We need to try another course that is unfamiliar to us. Maybe South Carolina would be good. We heard that the golfing is excellent there. We could go down there on Friday and return on Monday."

"How would you get there?" asked Ashley.

"Fly," said Matt. "We have a plane. We need to know if you and Anna would like to go with us."

"I hope you aren't getting tired of me," said Ashley.

"No, silly," replied Matt. "I'll never get tired of you. We are married. I hope you don't get tired of me."

"No, I'll never get tired of you either," replied Ashley. "You're so nice and have such good common sense. It will never happen."

"Thanks," said Matt.

"Okay, how would it work?" asked Ashley. "We have classes and all of that."

"Both of us have a Friday morning class," answered Matt. "We could leave Friday afternoon and return Sunday evening or Monday morning. Next semester, I will schedule Monday afternoon classes, if we like it."

"I'm free on Monday," said Ashley, "but you have something. We would have to leave Friday afternoon and return Sunday evening. Maybe we can work something out, but as of now, that's what we have to do."

Matt was deep in thought.

"What would you guys do?" asked Matt.

"That's easy," said Ashley. "We could shop. I love shopping, and am sure Anna would follow along. She rarely buys anything, because there is nothing around here that is good enough. That's the same way I feel."

"Then, I'll tell the General that Friday afternoon to Monday morning will be the itinerary," said Matt.

"Aren't you forgetting that you have Monday morning classes?" asked Ashley. "Remember that courses Monday through Friday are at the same time 9:00."

"You know I almost forgot; I was thinking about something else." said Matt. "There was some kind of conflict on Monday morning. So I gave in and said we could change Monday classed to afternoon. It might be for the rest of the current semester. It's always this, that, or something else."

"You just said that," said Ashley.

"It has a certain ring to it," replied Matt.

"You always give in," said Ashley with a smile.

"In the long run," said Matt, "that's the best way. Everyone knows that the professor or dean causing trouble was self-oriented and the next time, no one will give in. That works to our advantage in this case."

Matt gave the plan to the General, who was pleased and would ask Anna if she would like to visit Hilton Head Island in South Carolina.

"Anna probably knows by now," said Matt. "We're dealing with women, who are good at exchanging information."

"Did you have time to research the subject, that is, Hilton Head?" asked the General.

"I've already made a reservation at the Big Dune Hotel and Golf Courses, but I 'll check on it," said Matt. "The Big Dune is a new property, so I would say it's pretty good. I'll ask that student, named Michael Clark. He's having some difficulty with the course, so he will be more than willing to give his opinion."

"Michael Clark," said the General. "Is he related to my associate Mart Clark?"

"I have no clue," answered Mat. "I don't usually ask students about their families. There must be thousands of Clarks in this country."

The next morning, Matt asked Michael Clark about golf courses, hotels, and shopping on Hilton Head Island. Michael said he had one of those advertising brochures and would bring it the next morning. Matt came in to his office on Tuesday morning, even though he was not scheduled to come in. The brochure was in his box.

Matt took it to his office and looked through it. He noticed the Big Dune, Shelter Cove, Tanger Outlets, and an ad for Sun City Hilton Head developed by Del Webb. He wondered if the elder Clark had a residence in Sun City, which was a gated community with 3 golf courses.

After his last student for the day, Matt sat in his office and thought about this running around just to play golf. Why do people do this, just to play a couple of rounds of golf? Well, he thought that he would know in a few days. The Big Dune Hotel and Golf courses intrigued him. Two must be the magic number with the designer of the property. Two golf courses, two restaurants, two fitness centers, two pools, two bars, and two bedroom suites with all the amenities one could think of. It even had a place to store your clubs between visits, free of charge. Now that's a clever idea.

3

THE FIRST GOLF TRIP TO HILTON HEAD

The General, Anna, and Ashley were looking forward to their first visit to Hilton Head, but they left the details to Matt, including the golf course, the hotel, and the transportation facilities. The General volunteered to have the plane ready, including a flight plan. They would take two cars to the local airport, loaded with a set of clubs in each with 3 days of luggage for the trip. Both Matt and the General brought the special Maui clubs they acquired on a vacation to Hawaii. Matt calculated the time at 400 mph from New Jersey to Hilton Head to be 1 hour and 36 minutes for 655 miles, roughly one and a half hours. That seemed to be a reasonable flight, not too long and not too short.

The General's plane was waiting on the tarmac, ready for a safe trip to South Carolina. The aides parked their cars, and the passengers loaded themselves. The luggage was placed in the rear of the aircraft. Matt occupied the pilot's seat and the General took on the task of the co-pilot, or the First Officer, as it is currently known. The pilot is called the Captain. The co-pilot is not needed on the small modern aircraft. Matt started the engines and the twin fan jet engines fired up. The pilot had an artificial intelligence auto pilot that can take off and land and take care of flying the planes in between. Matt took off and landed manually.

"Matt, how fast will we be flying and how high," asked Anna, who wasn't used to flying. Matt was as cool as a cucumber.

"We'll be flying 400 miles per hour at 40,000 feet," said Matt. "The auto pilot is set. The flight is 655 miles and we will be taking a great circle route. We'll be there in 1 hour and 36 minutes. Music anyone?"

No one answered.

"The General will tell you about the trip," said Matt. "Don't worry, the plane is designed to fly high and fast, and can do that for the entire flight."

The General was so calm that he had fallen asleep.

"He's used to flying," said Matt. "Wake up General, your friends are waiting."

"I dreamed I was home in bed," said the General. "Would you like to hear about our trip?"

"Yes Sir." Said Ashley and Anna at the same time.

"We're going to stay in a golfing hotel to play a couple of rounds, and have made arrangements for you ladies to visit an outside designer mall named Shelter Cove, and an outlet mall called Tanger outlets," said the General. "Each of you has a credit card and you have authority to purchase anything you choose with no restrictions on what, number of items, and price. Both of you seem to be a little frugal for Matt and my taste. You will enjoy fine dining at the hotel for today, Saturday, and Sunday. We will return to New Jersey early on Monday. A car of some sort will pick us up at Hilton Head Airport and be at your disposal for the entire trip"

"Is that airport big enough to land?" asked Ashley. "It's small town."

"Without question," said Matt.

"Modern passenger aircraft can land and take off from remarkably small airports – we're talking about runways – and even the President's Air Force One has enough power to take off from a large postage stamp," said the General. "Long runways are used to carry heavy loads and for passenger comfort."

Everyone relaxed, including Matt, who was looking at a travel brochure for Hilton Head Island.

"What are you looking at?" said Ashley.

"Just looking at where the golf course is," answered Matt.

"It's next to the hotel, isn't it," asked the General.

"It is," said Matt. "We do not have an oceanfront – to the ocean. Is anyone sad about not being about not getting a suntan? We can always use the pools. They have two of them."

No one said anything.

The plane had a tail wind and arrived at the Hilton Head Airport in 1 hour and 30 minutes. The landing was smooth, and Matt was a careful pilot. After the plane landed, Matt taxied the plane to the General Aviation building. The hotel's limousine was waiting, only a few steps away. A driver's aid took care of the luggage and golf clubs. The driver headed for route 278, also known as Fording Island Road. In 5 miles or less, they were at the Big Dune Hotel and Golf Courses. There was no formal check-in, and the guests were escorted directly to their guest suite. Matt and the General went out to get the lay of the land and a glimpse of the course.

Matt and the General stopped at the area where golf carts were stored. A person was looking at them. Actually, he was staring at them.

"That gentleman who is staring at us looks familiar," said Matt.

"He does," said the General. "Let's take a closer look - right back at him."

Matt and the General walked over as the gentleman turned.

"Les, you old General," exclaimed Mark Clark, a four-star General of the U.S. military and an associate of the General, also a four-star General. "Are you guys following me?"

"Not at all, Mark" replied the General, "We're here to play a little golf and are just looking around. How about you?"

"I'm also here for some golf," said Mark Clark. "I live here now. Let's have a drink in the 19th hole."

The 19th hole is where golfers have a drink after they are finished playing a round of golf.

"You're on," said the General.

So the three gentlemen headed for the bar.

"I've figured it out," said Matt. "I'll tell you when we are finished with General Clark."

"What are you fine gentlemen doing in my hometown?" asked Clark, former Chairman of the Joint Chiefs of Staff.

"Les, I owe you a call and an explanation."

"I can't imagine what for," replied the General.

"You're meeting with me in the Pentagon – our last conversation," said Clark. "I was and I am on an important project, and I thought that the President was checking on me. He's that kind of guy, as you well know."

Matt looked at the General, as if to say, 'This is not a coincidence . This guy is following us and I wonder why. How would or could he know where we are. Perhaps it is the President, and he wants our help again.'

"Think about it Matt, " whispered the General. "By the time we finish our drink, you will have figured it out. You always do."

4

THE PLOT THICKENS

"What are you fine gentlemen doing in my hometown?" asked Mark Clark, former U.S. Army four-star General. "Les, I owe you a call and an explanation.

"I can't imagine what for," replied the General.

"It was our meeting in the Pentagon – our last conversation. I was and am in an important project, and I thought that the President was checking on me. I mentioned that already. How have you been, and what are you and your superb team working on?"

"Actually, we finished our project on the source of the pandemic, and we have been enjoying ourselves with a lot of golf. We're here to see how golfing is on Hilton Head Island. Our women are with us, and we're without any project to be concerned with. Are you free, as well?"

"Heavens no," said Clark. "I have a critical project on cybersecurity and terrorism and need an additional team to assist us. Does this project intrigue you? The U.S. Government is paying $200,000 per year along with expenses. My wife

Ann, you remember her, and I are living free of charge in Sun City, tax and expenses free. The cute little community and Hilton Head are where the action is suspected to be. We have a small home there, and have kept our home in the D.C. area. I hope you might be interested in a project like this."

"Matt and Ashley are academics and do not have total freedom. If they can work it out then I am quite certain they would be interested, and Anna and I are totally free for a new project," answered the General. "Our team is dispersed, except for Buzz Bunday, who is always available. However, it is important to state that we don't have a team without Matt and Ashley, who provide our intellectual power."

"We can live with the academics," said Clark. "Weekends and normal academic time off are all that I need."

"What do you think Matt?" asked the General. "You always have the plane at your disposal."

It was clear that the General wanted to do it. He liked to keep busy, and general officers shared a mutual bond. Probably, it was the case that they had to solve similar problems when they were on active duty.

"Cybersecurity and terrorism," said Matt, "sound very interesting. We do need an intellectual picker upper after the pandemic project. I think I can speak for Ashley. We are definitely interested."

"Quick question," said the General. "Do you have a son or grandson attending Matt's university?"

"I do," said Clark. "I have a grandson by the name of Michael Clark who is doing just that. I would keep him out of it, so that is as far as it goes. With him, nothing is secret, which is mandatory in this instance."

"Agreed," said Matt. "Will our work be totally U.S. secret?"

"It is," said Clark. "Even the President doesn't know about it completely, and the source of the project will not be known to you. Of course, If we have good results, we will duly inform the President and his Chief of Staff.

"That is the way we like it," replied the General.

"It's a little late now, and I know you are here for golf tomorrow," said Clark. "If so, may I join you? Do your better halves need some assistance? Ann is a top notch shopper."

"I think we had better ease into this," said Matt. "Ashley and Anna probably have their plans made. I fact, I don't think we should discuss it until we are headed home on Monday morning."

"That sounds prudent," said Clark. "We are sort of jumping to this. If you wish, Ann and I can scout out some property for you. There is more to it, and I know this is not the time to discuss it. Until we meet again, all I can say is that Sun City is a sleepy gated community with just about any activity you can imagine."

"What about pickle ball?" asked Matt.

"Where did you hear about that?" asked Clark.

"I saw it on TV," said Matt. "I don't even know what it is, but apparently a lot of seniors like it."

"We have pickle ball," said Clark, "and three golf courses and a lot of other things."

"By next weekend," replied the General. "Matt will know all we need to know about it."

"Okay, lets part now," said Clark. "Les and I will correspond via satellite pone. My cell, however, is 483-505-8995. Aren't you going to write it down?"

"No need," said the General. "Matt will remember it."

The men agreed on a time for tomorrow's golf, and Clark walked off. Matt and the General proceeded back to their suite. Matt looked over at the General. He had a twinkle in his eyes.

When Matt and the General got back to the suite, the first thing that Anna said was, "You must have met some bathing suit girls."

"No," said General. "We met someone but it wasn't girls; it was an old Army buddy of mine, and we had a lot to talk about. We'll let you know about the conversation on the flight home."

"Let's eat," said Ashley. "Us girls are hungry."

The group had a wonderful dinner, and agreed that Hilton Head had a lot to offer. They decided to retire early, because their tee time was early.

As they walked out, a couple seated in the next table watched their every move. The woman said, "I've never seen two couples that are so perfectly matched. They must be European Aristocracy. The men are tanned, so they don't have to work." Her husband, said, "They are American. You didn't notice how they used their eating utensils. But, there is no doubt that they are quite wealthy."

5

GOLF WITH THE GENERAL

The General and Mark Clark arranged a 6:30 tee time, and Matt was pleased that they had. Hilton Head Island in the morning is a wonderful place. The sky is blue, the birds are chirping, and the people are friendly. The ladies had planned an old fashioned shopping spree and an exotic lunch at the Olive Garden. Matt hoped that Ashley would spend more on her clothes. She didn't seem to care, so there wasn't much he could say or do.. Perhaps shopping with Anna would change all of that.

Matt and the General skipped breakfast, hoping they could grab something after the 18th hole.

The course was beautiful and well-manicured. The round of golf was enjoyable., and the General and General Clark were engaged in an active conversation for the entire time. Two ex-military men are a good pair. Clark said that being a General was a pleasing and rewarding experience.

Being Chairman of the Joint Chiefs of Staff was a constant irritation, and he was more than pleased when it was over. They had breakfast in the hotel and the restaurant was a replica of the Skillets Restaurant, destroyed in a massive fire in Hilton Head's Coligny Plaza area. Coligny Plaza was in a residential section, in contrast to most of HHI, as it was commonly referred to, was upscale gated communities, similar in concept to Sun City. Most communities had an expensive hotel and a golf course. As one might expect, the various golf courses were in competition for golfers. The Coligny Plaza area had a Piggly Wiggly grocery store, and the General was anxious to try some Old Trenton Crackers, a brand of oyster crackers popular in the southeast. Incidentally, people loved to refer to the Piggly Wiggly as the Pig, with a slight grin on their face.

The three fine gentlemen were escorted to a great table overlooking the Atlantic Ocean, and nothing could be finer than to be in Hilton Head Island on a leisurely Saturday morning. The General asked about the project, as General Clark had hoped he would.

"We have a terrible crisis in this country, and most people do not know it, are ignoring it, or hoping it will go away," said Clark. "When something unfortunate happens, people are afraid for a few weeks, and then slowly, the crisis seems to go away. Typically, they know we have a serious national problem, and think the President and various branches of the Government will take care of it. Well, they don't and the crisis becomes bigger than before."

"Most people, including myself, don't completely understand the crisis" said Matt. "So they ignore it. When is the last time a bomb incident or a shooting occurred. Most people forget how, when, and where in a few days. I heard a man talking in the lobby yesterday evening. Apparently, there was a bunch of young men walking in the Coligny area like they owned the place, and people had to get out of their way in the walking area. The man continued by saying that most people must have thought they were Hispanic, and accepted it as young cultural behavior. He said that he had worked in Iran and other middle-eastern countries for ten years, and he was sure they were Iranian. He wanted to speak to them in their native language, but his wife told him not to do it."

"Who knows what those men are doing today?" said the General. "I think we see your point."

"We have pinpointed this location – HHI – as a terrorist hotspot," said Clark. "There are several reasons that I can delineate. First, entry to the country around here is easy. There are fishermen for a few hundred terrorist dollars will bring them in. Secondly, the people that live here are older – many elderly – and they don't like controversy of any sort. If something does happen, they will probably ignore it. Third, this is a tourist area and many visitors happen, in fact, to look different. They are from just about any country in the world. Fourth, rich people do not like to get involved with other people's business, and lastly, the residences are relatively far apart, so a terrorist can come and go with impunity."

"Just because they can doesn't guarantee that they will," said Matt. "Do you have evidence that they are here?"

"We do," said Clark. "There is a moderately sized home on the right side of Fording Island Road, that is Route

278, just before the Shelter Cove shopping area. The owner rents his front yard for Christmas tree and pumpkin sales. Several other people do this. As the story goes, the family on the wife's side needed money because of a major medical problem, and the husband did not want to sell, so he puts it up for sale at a ridiculous price, so high that no one would bid on it or even look at it. A young lawyer, supposedly representing a client, agreed to pay for it, and the real estate office was obligated to accept the offer. At the high price, the tax rate went up astronomically, and the lawyer paid the tax bill also. So some patriotic person in the tax office called the FBI, and we are here with an explicit assignment to find out what's going on. Here is what I've done so far, and remember, I am working alone on this – at least so far. I didn't and don't know explicitly how to find out, so I contacted military intelligence, and subsequently a contract office in administration, and we now have a team of six people on the case. Here is what they have determined so far. The home has been totally remodeled on the inside, and the old furnishings were removed. The insides wee replaced with luxury furnishings. The owner drives a Cadillac Escalade. His wife wears one of those Muslim hijabs and drives a Toyota. They have two Internet connections, both 5G, and all messages are encrypted. The coded messages were sent to the NSA and they haven't come up with anything except that the cryptographic methods are changed frequently and the methods are first rate. The woman goes to a bread restaurant where she meets other mothers. They have removed their hijabs, and jabber away in a language that one of the team says is Spanish. Another member of the team knows Spanish like the back of her hand, and says it is not Spanish, but sounded middle-eastern. We have recorded their conversation, using a couple of member of the team who know Arabic and said the conversation was definitely in Farsi. They talk about school and things seem to be okay, except for the woman from the remodeled home, whose son is doing poorly in math. The women are happy with their lives. Other women in the restaurant think they are Hispanics riding the money trail, but our team is sure they are middle-eastern. We thought that the removal of hijabs was significant. One of the ladies is a nurse, trained in the States and is married to a middle easterner. She helps with the kids by taking care of medical things. She was trained as an ICU nurse. Another key point is that they do not talk about what their husbands do for a living or even what they do all day. One of the husbands may be a professor at the University of South Carolina in Hilton Head. There are some new luxury apartments near Shelter Cove in Hilton Head and most of the middle-eastern women and their families live there. The family on Fording Island Road seems to be the leader, but it is not clear why it does not live in the apartments."

"The last point is clear," said Matt. "They may be living on Fording Island Road so they can do things they couldn't do otherwise. Perhaps, that set of things is related to the data communications. Was there anything on the ladies use of the data communication facilities?"

"They all use messaging," said Clark. "Someone of the team said he thought they did not even know email and were not interested in the Internet. The ex-American nurse was asking questions and then used the conclusions she drew from Internet access. She told them they should learn about the computer stuff, and finally gave up."

"We have to meet and make a plan," said the General. "Before we leave for New Jersey, we will give you our plan. One question: How long do you think it will be until the terrorist operation will take place? We have some high-powered women to call upon, and we have an ex-associate on the Hilton Head police force?"

"His name is Harry Steevens and his quick thinking saved us from getting killed." said Matt. "The man is very capable. He pulled out a Beretta from his ankle holster in the Airport and plugged the guy. At the ankle level, guns are not detected in airports. I'll try to contact him."

The three gentlemen enjoyed their breakfast but didn't like the situation. The General, on the other hand, was pleased.

6

THE HILTON HEAD MASTER PLAN

"What do you think, Matt," said the General as they returned to their suite.

"It appears to be an interesting project," said Matt. "I'm quite concerned about whether my off time will be enough for this project."

"We can organize our operation so that we are in control how much time we can allocate to the government work," said the General. "But before we can do my scheduling, we should develop an idea of precisely what we will have to do."

"Okay, I'll go along with that," said Matt. "We need to find out what is going on at the Fording Island Road residence. I think that may be where the problem lies."

"You will think of something, Matt," said the General. 'You always do."

"Right," said Matt. "That's what you always say."

Both Matt and the General cleaned up, and decided to sit on the balcony overlooking the Atlantic Ocean. The General looked over at Matt, whose brain was going a mile a minute. Matt went in and came back with a note pad and a pencil – the kind normally found by the hotel telephone. Here is what Matt scribbled on the pad:

- Fording Island Road
- What's going on inside
- Math student
- A good-looking female
- Tutor the boy
- Kids nowadays have special tablet computers
- Kid will come in with one
- Most if not all kids have the same model
- Have a couple of copies made of same model
- Add visual and auditory components to the tablets
- Exchange when the kid goes to the bathroom
- Feed him a lot of Coca Cola
- In the first session, have tutor explain he will do better after drinking coke
- Kid goes to the rest room
- Tutor exchanges tablets
- Continue for several sessions
- Need more than modified tablet
- Do this with several kids
- Then pull out all but target saying they are okay
- How to get kid to tutor:
    - Contact kid's school teacher

- Have her send message to parents saying kid needs help with math
- Arrange with our tutor

Matt handed the list to the General, who looked at the list.

"What if the guy – the enemy – has someone watch the kid?" said the General. "I think the kind of person we're dealing with would put a watch on the kid."

"Distract him," said Matt.

"How?" replied the General

"That's easy," said Matt. "Have a woman come in with a low neckline, real low. Even devout Muslims like to look. Contact Harry, and have him come in with a nice looking woman."

"He probably already has a few of them," said the General. "We can pay them. Can you contact that guy Harry to see where he is?"

"His name is Harry Steevens," answered Matt. " Remember the name Harry comes from Gregory pronounced Greg-hari.

"Yeah, now I remember him," said the General. "We also need to talk with Clark's 6 person team. Want to talk tonight or tomorrow?"

We should give Clark's team a chance to get accustomed to having a bunch of helpers," said Matt. "How about next weekend. Anyway we are behind with our golf."

"Sounds okay," said the General. "I'll contact Clark, and maybe you can contact Gregory – I mean Harry."

<<<<<<<<<<<<>>>>>>>>>>

Matt got a call from Ashley. "I was looking at the TV in one of the shops and there is a Heritage Festival going on right now on Hilton Head, and a golfer made a shot within snapping distance of an alligator. They must be used to alligators around here."

"Did they show it on TV?" asked Matt.

"They did," replied Ashley. "How was your morning?"

"The golf was great, but the General's buddy Mark Clark had some interesting news. I'll tell you later."

"What size shoes do you wear?" asked Ashley. "It's nine and a half, isn't it?"

"You have something in mind, don't you?" asked Matt. "It is nine and a half, I don't need anything."

"We're at Cole Hahn's at Tanger outlets," said Ashley. "You can return them."

"I hope they don't have my size," replied Matt. "What would you and Anna like for dinner?"

"We had a salad for lunch," said Ashley. "So it doesn't matter. Do you want to hear something?

"Of course," said Matt.

"There was a table nearby filled with a bunch of women. They had slightly darker skin. Anna thought they were Hispanic, living off the land, so to speak. She said they were speaking Spanish, but I know Spanish like the back of my hand, and it wasn't Spanish. You know, they were from the middle-east. I've had many middle-eastern students and the ladies at the next table looked like they were from Iran. What do you think? You can figure out anything."

"They were from Iran," said Matt. "I can depend on your judgment. See you and Anna when you get here."

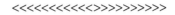

A half hour later, Ashley and Anna arrived the Big Dune Hotel and Golf Courses with packages and two immense smiles.

"We had a great day," said Anna. "I never thought shopping could be so much fun. Shelter Cove was the right size; large enough to enjoy looking at just about everything and small enough that you didn't want to leave. Tanger Outlet was a buyer's paradise."

Ashley just smiled and Matt knew she had a good time. Matt's shoes were only $100 at the Cole Haan shop and size 9 ½ was perfect.

"We have a lot to talk about," said the General. "So let's get freshened up and head downstairs."

The Big Dune's restaurant was indeed grand. The Maitre d' was attentive and, as usual, Matt chose the seating. The General, Ashley, and Anna knew what he was doing. He wanted to be seated so they couldn't be observed or heard. It was s sure sign that they had something important to talk about.

The minute they sat down, Ashley said, "That Maitre d' and waiter are Iranian. I'd bet a million dollars on it."

"I'd bet two million dollars that they are from Brooklyn," said the General with a laugh. "You guys are really humorous. What would a couple of Iranians be doing in Hilton Head, South Carolina?"

"Spying," said Matt.

"That's what I was afraid of." said the General. "Once these groups infiltrate a domain, they are everywhere infiltrating every avenue of our daily lives. Matt, will you tell the ladies what has come up?"

"Sure," said Matt. "The General and I went down to look at the golf course and ran into one of his Army associates–note that I am not saying buddies – by the name of Mark Clark, who was also a general, now retired. Clark arranged with our General to play our round of golf at 6:30 this morning. Apparently, Clark is down here to look into some terrorist activity similar to the 911 attack. Remember, after 911, there was some talk that another was planned. This was before the American military killed Osama bin Laden, and his brother stated there was going to be another attack. That's really why Clark is here. There was some intelligence that the terrorists were in and around Hilton Head, as this is a hot spot for middle eastern activity of a questionable nature. They have a team of U.S. Government people under cover to resolve the situation. To me, this means remove the threat. His team doesn't have much firepower, and we just happened to appear on the scene. We have a good reputation, and Clark just jumped at the chance of getting us. I believe there is more to our meeting and it is not pure chance, but that is an issue for another meeting. The General and I implicitly agreed that we would address the problem. We would have special U.S. Government power, U.S. Government IDs, and as much money as we need. We have the authorization to make a plan and build a group. We have a reason to come down to Hilton Head, ostensibly to play golf. This is a common thing that people with enough money do. The terrorists have some property on Fording Island Road that is a U.S. highway 278 that you probably rode on. The circumstances are such that we need to know what is going on there. I have conceptualized a plan using a math tutor from the team six, which is Clark's team, and use this as a way of getting the information we need. The plan is more complicated than we should discuss here. We need people that will work for us and not necessarily be in team six. We have figured it would be you Ashley, and Anna, and possibly a person named Harry Steevens, who I hear is now with the Hilton Head Police Department. Initially, he could be a distraction as the tutor and a kid will undoubtedly be under surveillance. To interject some fun into all this, I conceptually view Harry with an attractive young lady with a very low cut neckline. Everyone kind of knows that most Iranian men love booze, hamburgers, and American women. As for now, we should make a plan to come down to Hilton Head for golf and have a planning meeting with team six. By the way, the Iranian women that you saw in the restaurant imply that their husbands have something to do with all of this. Already, some hard evidence has surfaced. We will give more information on the flight home. The maître d' and the waiter have us under scrutiny, and as you have noticed, I sit facing the other way, and hesitate when they are close. The maître d' in particular has eyeballed us practically every minute, since the number of guests is relatively low. They may have photographed us but they got no audio. I'm sure that the big boss will have heard about us by tomorrow morning. I do not believe they know anything about our team, since they undoubtedly came in to the States via Hilton Head and don't know much about New Jersey, Washington D.C., England and the Royals, and Switzerland. Our food is on its way, so let's continue this in the suite or on the plane."

Ashley and the General ordered steak, Anna ordered chicken, and Matt chose fish. As far as the drinks were concerned, the General had a double scotch, Anna had a martini, Matt had an O'doul's alcohol free beer, and Matt told Ashley to order a virgin Mary, and asked if the waiter knew what it was. If he knew a virgin Mary was a Bloody Mary without the vodka, then he had been here for awhile. Ashley asked subsequently if he knew what a virgin Mary was, and if he didn't, then he hadn't been here very long.

The dinner prepared by the Big Dune kitchen was delicious and was thoroughly enjoyed. The conversation was lively after Matt had finished.

On the way out, the eyes of other patrons were on them. A woman said, "I can't figure them out. They listened intently when the younger man was talking and then lightened up afterwards, and they had a good time." Her husband replied, "It interested me also. The older guy acted like the boss, but clearly the young guy was in control. I thought they might be in real estate, since it would be difficult to talk that long about traditional business." The woman said, "I think he is a professor, because he could talk so long." The husband said, "No one fell asleep."

<<<<<<<<<<>>>>>>>>>>

The General called Mark Clark that evening and said that he and his team would fly down the following Friday.

They would arrive around dinner-time, and they needed a pick up, so the enemy would not know where they come from and why. Golf was planned for the weekend, as reason for the trip.

Matt and the General played a round of golf on Sunday, stored their Maui clubs at the Big Dune Hotel and Golf Courses, and flew home late that afternoon.

PART II
THE PROJECT

7

BACK TO NEW JERSEY

On the flight from Hilton Head to New Jersey, Matt set the speed at 400 mph at 40,0000 feet, and they all relaxed, happy in the knowledge that the weekend was over.

Before they left, Matt called Harry.

"Harry," said Matt. 'Whatever happened to you after you went off with Amelia?"

"Sorry I didn't call you Matt," said Harry Steevens, former New Jersey state patrolman. "She said she would get me a good job in the government, and she did. I was behind a desk one hundred percent of the time. I got very good pay, and my reviews were outstanding. But, I was bored to death and resigned. By then, she was gone somewhere. I never found out. I called a friend from the New Jersey State Patrol who had gone to Hilton Head, because they were reorganizing the police department and were paying good money. She got me a top position. So, that's where I am."

"How about you, Matt?" asked Harry. "I thought of you afterwards and was too ashamed to call you."

"It's the same, Harry," replied Matt. "Still teaching and the general and I pick up some high-level jobs from time to time. In fact, that's why I called you. Are you free for some part-time work? The pay is phenomenal, and the hours are short. I think there is little danger, if any, and your experience would be invaluable to us."

"Okay, you're on, buddy," said Harry. "Just give me a call. You, no doubt, have my land line phone number and police number. My cell is 843-505-2668. You probably need a bank number and I'll give that to you when we meet."

"We are in Hilton Head now," said Matt, "and we will be back next Friday in the late afternoon. We plan a meeting for late that day, and it would be worthwhile for you to keep the evening free."

"I will Matt," said Harry. "Friday is my day off in the current rotation."

"Harry," said Matt. "I have put you on the team and the honorarium will be substantial. Over and out, Harry"

"You too," said Harry.

The flight to New Jersey was exceedingly smooth. The General started the conversation.

"You ladies might not know what happened to us, so I'll just repeat everything," said the General. "Matt and I went down to look at the golf course. We ran into General Mark Carter. Both of you have met him. Whether the meeting was happen stance, or he looked at our flight plan and drew the most logical conclusion, we might never know. He could have had someone call all of the hotels with golf courses, saying he or she was the FBI or something like that, and got the information about our reservation and our future plans. He has a big and important project, now that he is retired, as I am. The Government is paying for everything, and it is a very serious matter. The country and the world are still reeling from the 911 incident. The Government was informed about an unusual real estate transaction, and there is something strange and unusual resulting from the purchase of a home on Floating Island Road on the right hand side heading toward Coligny Plaza. They have a strange set of 5G communication lines. So far, Clark has no Intel on that occurrence. Clark and his wife have purchased a home in a gated community named Sun City. The residence was purchased with Government money, and we think we will be expected to do the same. We have no knowledge of this unusual procedure, but whatever they want us to do is satisfactory to us. It would be easy to have terrorists enter the country at Hilton Head Island. There are a lot of reasons, mostly related to tourism and the older-age population, and rich people generally don't pay attention to affairs outside their domain. The honorarium will be two hundred thousand dollars per year plus expenses. Our personal lives should not be adversely affected by this project. Matt will continue this narrative."

"We need to know what is going on in the Floating Island Road residence," said Matt. "Clark already has a team of six people ready to go. They do not seem to know what to do, so we will take over from there. We are going to have the kick off meeting next Friday afternoon. I have an approach that I think will be appropriate. I'll talk about it later, on our next trip down to Hilton Head.

8

ACTION ON FLOATING ISLAND ROAD

His name is Atalus, and he headed the middle-eastern terrorist team. Osama bin Laden had said, before being dramatically killed by American military forces, that there would be another attack on American soil, and it would be impossible to detect it beforehand. The terrorist team had infiltrated the country at Hilton Head Island, in a pre-determined location. Most of the terrorists were engineers and scientists, and they specialized in aerodynamics and computer science, especially artificial intelligence. The team contracted with a young American lawyer, just out of law school, to handle all legal transactions. Atalus would handle al business transactions, as well as, employee salaries and expenses.

Atalus had contacts at all luxury hotels with an emphasis on those that specialized in golf, which was the usual excuse for most American dealing. Julia was a middle easterner at the Big Dune Hotel and Golf Courses. She looked American and was good at languages, and was an administrative assistant to the management. Julia was one of several contacts that reported to Atalus, who used his real name and was quite open about his interpersonal transactions. When a rich looking man checked in, usually with a team of employees, the administrative assistant simply called Atalus and him gave the registration details. Julia was paid $10,000 per month handled with a cash payment. Here is a typical interaction.

"Mr. Atalus, we have a team of two men and two women checking into the big Dune, suite 5 on the 8th floor," said Julia. "They brought golf clubs and conventional luggage." "Tell me about the ages and looks of the customers," said Atalus.

"Older man, older woman, young man, and younger woman. Men are very tanned and the women are dressed casually with stylish clothes."

"Thanks, Julia," said Atalus. "Payment at noon on Friday at the reception area in front of the ladies rest room. We are using the same runner."

"Thank you, Sir," said Julia.

Later in the day, Atalus called the Maitre d' at the Big Dune Hotel.

"Big Dune one, any new customers?" asked Atalus.

"Yes, Sir," said the person with code name Big Dune one. "There is a group of two men and two women. The men are golfers, athletic looking, sun tanned, and straight up like military. The young man ran the show. He selected the seats for the group, including himself. He faced away from me and stopped talking when I came near their table. I could not record anything or tape anything visual."

It was the same with Big Dune two, the waiter. The waiter said he felt the young man looked at him with a fierce stare. He felt the young woman was recording and taping him. The diners were pleasant with each other – older man to older woman and young man to young woman. The younger couple appeared to be married. The young woman placed her purse on the table, and it was a Dooney and Bourke, usually modified for secret taping.

"What do you think, Big Dune one?" asked Atalus. "Are they trouble or government?"

"They are not government," said Big Dune one, "but they might be trouble. The older man had scotch, the older woman had a martini, the younger man had O'doul'S, and the young woman ordered a virgin Mary, and the waiter said he didn't know what it was. All Americans know what a virgin Mary is. Big Dune Two made a mistake, he should have said he knew what a virgin Mary is and then he should have asked the bartender. We are supposed to be Americans."

"Keep an eye on him," said Atalus. "Thanks, you will get the usual $10,000 on Friday outside the ladies room in the lobby."

Atalus left his computer room and attended to his family. His wife answered a question about the son's math studies and remarked the boy needed a tutor. Atalus said nothing.

Atalus was exceedingly careful about almost everything that went on outside of his home and over which he had no direct control. He had an American runner, he called Joe, who followed his kids, wife, and members of his team. Joe daily followed Atalus' son to grammar school, his wife to the hairdresser, and his wife and her friends to social places, such as the bread store where they talked and enjoyed American coffee. Joe made it plainly known he was observing the person in which he was interested. Atalus and Joe were interested in anyone who interacted with his wife and her friends. Atalus' team, excluding himself, lived in the new luxury apartments at the end of the Hilton Head city park. Atalus' sponsor owned all of the apartments and automobiles. The sponsor was unknown personally to Atalus, who was more of an organizational and technical leader.

Atalus studied at Harvard and graduated before he enrolled in the Master of Science program in Management at MIT, where he graduated with the highest honors. He was as smart as a tick and could remember the smallest details.

Atalus' team was not recruited by him but was subsequently approved by him. An American lawyer made all payments of a substantial nature and approved all agreements. The whole project was the responsibility of a professor in New York City's Chinatown or Boston's Chinatown, but Atalus did not know whether or not he was Chinese.

Atalus personally felt the project was organized and funded by Osama bin Laden's brother, who lives in Afghanistan.

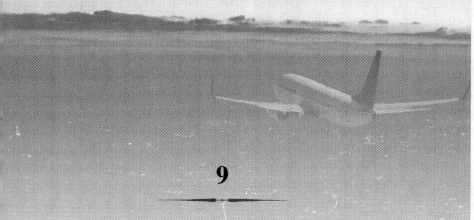

9

THE PROJECT'S FIRST MEETING

Former four-star General Mark Clark scheduled the project's first meeting in a small conference room in the Big Dune's restaurant. Matt had Harry sweep the room for electronic bugs just before the start. Actually, the sweep was finished one minute before the six-o'clock start.

Clark covered the purpose of the meeting and the persons involved. The six people in his section of the total of 12 people were six government employees. They were familiar with the terrorist situation, but had no experience with problems that were similar with the current one. The people were:

Nancy Small – Government statistician
Max Smith – electrical engineering
Joyce Johnson – human resources
Al Thomas – geologist
Dick Hurling – management

Michelle Harbinger – school teacher

General Les Miller introduced his team that consisted of:

Matt Miller – math professor
Ashley Miller – analyst and drama professor
Marguerite Purgoine – analyst and writer
Harry Steevens – Hilton Head policeman and CIA officer
Mary Brown – Hilton Head policewoman
Sir Charles Bunday – British secret service and international affairs Les Miller mentioned that he was also a General officer, as was General Clark, and that Sir Bunday was a specialist in international affairs that was a significant part of the current project, and that he, the speaker, was generally known as The General.

The General was a little tired and Matt noticed it, and took over the chair of their aspect of the problem.

"We have extensive experience with ill-defined national and international situations," Said Matt. "Although my associate, the General, has in his background a bachelor's degree in math, he also has a master's in computer science, and a PhD in international affairs. This is why, the two Generals are a productive team."

The Clark team just looked at each other. They knew that they were teamed with more than competent companions.

"We suspect we have a terrorist situation that is being run out of a house on Floating Island Road. There are some very high-speed communication lines in and out of the house that is unusual in Hilton Head. Actually, they are unusual for any place. Quite by accident, we have observed several relatively attractive women that removed their hijabs and were talking in the bread store. They looked to be Hispanic living the good life while their husbands worked for a living. We determined, quite by accident, that they were not speaking Spanish but rather a middle-eastern language, probably Farsi. We don't exactly know where they live, but it's probably the new luxury apartments near to Shelter Cove. We don't believe that they can afford the apartments. So something is going on. Before Osama bin Laden was killed by U.S. Armed Forces, he said there will be another attack. Something major is going on and we don't know how, when, and why."

"It's impossible," said Max Smith, the electrical engineer. "There is not enough engineering knowledge among any of the terrorists."

"Not true," said Matt. "During the course of the project, we will show you how. Let's take a break."

Matt whispered to Ashley, "We need to get inside that house on Floating Island Road, and I have an idea. We can use a tutor and an electric tablet that kids use to learn math. We can load it with visual and verbal capability. The kid comes in with his, and we switch. He takes the loaded one home and it collects sound and visual information without anyone knowing it. He comes back for his next lesson, and the tutor switches again. This goes on until we have the information we need. Then the tutor tells the father that his kid is up to the rest of the kids. I've heard that Iranian fathers will do anything to have educated kids, especially the oldest boy. We can do it at the coffee shop. The tutor loads the kid with Coke and then he has to go to the bathroom. The switch is made when he is in the rest room. Kids love Coke."

"What if someone is watching the kid, so he doesn't get kidnapped, or something like that," replied Ashley. "Sounds like a very good idea except for that."

"I'll think of something." Said Matt.

During the break, Matt said to Nancy, "I've been looking at you." Nancy smiled and replied, "Matt, I've been looking at you, too."

"I'm married," said Matt.

"I'm married, also," replied Nancy.

"I have a small plan," said Matt. "We need to know what's going on inside that house, and I have an idea. There's a young boy in there, and we can arrange to have a tutor, or he won't move on to the next level in school. We can have Michelle arrange for the tutor. That would be you, because you look the best. Michelle will not know the whole story, because it is necessary to have this operation compartmentalized. Next, we get a several kid's electronic tablets and have them modified for sound and visual data acquisition. I know someone in military intelligence who can do it. They can do anything with electronics. The teacher is Mary Brown, who is on our team as a part-time policewoman. She will prepare a note for the mother, who should tell it to the father. We think he is the leader of the terrorists. The mother, father, and kid arrangement will be a disguise to get the kid's tablet that will be supplied by the school district, for foreign residents. The mother will call you to arrange for a session with you, and Mary Brown will supply you with the math learning materials. During the first session, you will explain the use of the tablet and give him home work on the tablet and press a secret set of action to start the running of the subversive components. We will give you a time schedule for the intercepted data acquisition. The plan is simple so far. During operation, the kid will do his homework, as usual. The tablet will store visual information and sound for an appropriate length of time. The kid comes back with his tablet loaded with information for us, and you will switch with him, so we can get the data. Now, things get touchy. You will be watched, and the kid will be trailed by a person named Joe who will watch your every move. You have to fill the kid with Coke and tell him that he will do better with his math if he drinks lots of Coke. Maybe it does. You will have him do some trivial thing on the tablet and then have to pee. He won't want to pee on his new tablet, so he will leave it with you. You want to switch tablets, so we have to distract Joe. Harry will come in with Mary, disguised with a very low neckline and be relatively active from a visual point of view. Joe will watch the demonstration, as a normal person would, and you switch tablets. It will be analogous to a black box. We can read the black box and we will have our information. The General knows a professor in Boston who will be able to interpret the information. We've used him before, and I have even flown him between New Jersey and Boston. Do you understand the plan, so far?"

"I do," said Nancy. "It is an ingenious plan."

"Will your husband okay this plan?' asked Matt.

"Of course," answered Nancy. "He's on the practice squad of the Boston Blues, and seldom plays, but is hoping for a major role with the team."

"I think we can get 4 or 5 kids math tablets – sometimes called pads – in a couple of days, and your electrical engineer named Max Swift, can handle the electronics," said Matt. "No one will know anyone else's role. Can you handle the plan and want to do it?" asked Matt.

"I do want to do it," said Nancy. "Thanks for the opportunity."

"Your General Clark," said Matt, "will handle the details. After we have more information, we can move on with the project."

Matt described the plan to the General who explained it to General Clark. The team was on its way.

10

GETTING THE GENERAL'S TEAM IN PLACE

The people in General Clark's team were first class. Nancy Small handled the tutoring and the interchange of the student's tablet went without a hitch. Max Smith was a top-notch electrical engineer, and two black boxes were available by Wednesday. Atalus, the father, was amazingly responsive to the teacher's request for tutoring. The reason was obvious. A man's prime interest in life was his first son, because a person's key to heaven was how well the first-born son did in life. Harry Steevens and Mary Brown thoroughly enjoyed being lovers at the coffee shop, since that was what they were in the first place.

The language recorded on the tablets will not be English, so Matt decided to call his friend Allen Weinberg in Boston.

Allen was a computer science professor, and his specialty was languages.

"Hi Allen," said Matt. "How have you been?"

"Matt," said Allen. "I haven't heard from you in a while and wondered if you were still around."

"I am," said Matt. "We're still in New Jersey, and I am still teaching math at the university. We have an important problem in Hilton Head and wondered if you could help us."

"Hilton Head," said Allen. "I know it well. My brother and his wife live there, and we often visit. He's an aeronautical specialist from design to construction, and his wife teaches at USCB,"

"I don't know what USCB is," said Matt.

"It stands for the University of South Carolina Beaufort," said Allen. "She teaches hospitality in the new facility that they have recently completed. My wife and I visit during every school break. It is really nice there, and we know the place like the back of my hand. Do you still fly that new airplane you call the Little Man?"

"Sure do," said Matt. "We're working on an important terrorist problem and have data to decipher. It is middle-eastern, probably Farsi."

"I can do it," said Allen. "I'm free for a week starting Friday. Is that good with you?"

"It's fine Allen," replied Matt. "Do you want me to pick you and your wife up in Little Man from Logan Airport?"

"Just tell me what time I should be at General Aviation on Thursday evening, or later on Friday morning," said Allen.

"Okay Allen," replied Matt, "I'll call you back in a half hour and let you know. We will pay you very well, and it will be worth your effort."

"Doesn't matter, Matt," said Allen. "We will be there. I will wait for your call."

"Sir, we have to get Allen Weinberg down here," said Matt. "I'm sure you remember him, since you never forget anything."

"Thank you, Matt," answered the General. "I usually don't, but please tell me what the schedule is."

"Your team is scheduled down on Friday," said Matt, "and Weinberg if free on Thursday. He will bring his wife, as he has relations in Hilton Head. Your plane holds four passengers – so I guess we can make it with the rest of the team. We can fly to Boston, pick them up and then fly to Hilton Head. Maybe Ashley and I can leave early for our universities. Is it all right with you to fly to Boston on Thursday, PM, and then fly on to Hilton Head?"

"Sounds okay with me, Matt," said the General. "Set it up and let me know, so I can file a flight plan. Also, I'll do the reservation at the Big Dune Hotel and Golf Courses. We're going to need a car. Let me talk to Clark about that. When I talk to you next, I'll let you know what he says. He's living in Sun City, and I'll have to ask about that also. I'm surprised that he hasn't had a problem of some kind down there. He always had problems."

"That he does, said Matt.

Matt arranged for a Boston pickup for the Weinberg's on Thursday and a final destination of Hilton Head Island. The General asked Clark to look into housing at Sun City, and Clark stated that an outright purchase would give them the security and privacy they needed. The General also needed an eight-passenger SUV and was advised to look in Bluffton, a suburb of Hilton Head, for delivery at the airport. The only vehicle available for immediate purchase was an eight passenger Chevrolet Suburban in dark blue. It didn't look like a government car, and the General thought that might be an advantage.

"Let's set up a meeting of both teams on Friday," said the General. "We can put Allen Weinberg to work on Friday and hope to get out for a round of golf."

"The set up time of the black boxes by the electrical engineer, so Weinberg can work on the data, should take some time," said Matt. " I'm very glad our clubs are stored at the Big Dune."

The Little Man aircraft landed at Hilton Head Airport at 6:30 pm on Thursday, and the 2021 Chevy Suburban was waiting at the General Aviation building. They dropped Weinberg and his wife at the brother's home, and in minutes were checking in to the Big Dune. They arranged for a meeting for the next morning at 10:00 am.

11

THE BLACK BOXES

The next morning, Friday, at 9:00 am, Allen Weinberg and Max Swift, the electrical engineer from Cark's team, were hard at work on the black boxes. They had two of them to look at. The black box from the son's first math tablet was not very useful, because the kid kept it to himself, and mostly represented a lot of playing around with a new toy. There were 2 or 3 background sounds that mentioned Chinatown in New York and an airport in New Hampshire. Max, who was brought up in Portsmouth, New Hampshire remembered there was an Air Force Base, named Pease Air Fore Base that had been closed and then re-opened, and they released about 1,000 acres for wildlife research. It was paved with some small buildings and other things. Trees and other foliage enclosed the paved area and a plane could land there without anyone seeing it. The land was totally accessible by paved roads. There is plenty of open land in New Hampshire, so no one paid any attention to it. Max called his mother, who still lived there.

"Hi Mom, this is Max," said Max. "How are you and Dad? I have a very quick question."

"Well, what is it," said Mrs. Swift.

"What ever happened to Pease Air Base?" asked Max.

"I was closed, then opened, and then re-purposed," said Mrs. Swift. "It seems to take care of air re-fueling. Now. Dad was up there, looking for hunting places, and said it was filled with a lot of fuel tanks. There were many signs saying it was military property. There weren't any fences and you could walk right in. Dad said he wouldn't dare go in there."

"Is that it?" asked Max.

"That's all I know," said Mrs. Swift. "How are you?"

"Good, Mom," said Max. "Call you later."

"What's this Chinese stuff?" asked Max, who had already established himself as an electronics expert and had everyone's respect.

"I've heard about this guy, a university professor or dean, who seems to be involved with terrorist activity," replied Allen. 'I think we thought he was involved with financing. Let's have a look at the other black box."

"We have good results here, Allen," said Max. "Awe have a photo of this guy Atalus' computer screen. or should I say multiple computers, and some text? He's sending these guys to New Hampshire to fix or to find something. I would love to know what they are fixing, and they are finding. Do you know where they live? Perhaps, we can have someone tail them. Do you know this guy Harry? He seems like a real tough guy. Can you call him?"

"I'd better pass this by Matt or the General," said Allen. "Let me try to find one of them."

Allen called Matt and got a surprising response.

"Our plan is to combine the two teams to form a system that is creative and open to ideas," said Matt. "I'll call Harry and his associate, Mary Brown, asking them to look into the situation. We have another issue here, and I would say that we have to determine the movement of the complete set of people involved. We should check out the ladies, when they congregate. What I'm getting at is if they perform a terrorist act, they are going to want to escape. The question is how. Thanks for the good work so far, Allen. See you later in the day. We're golfing, since it is our underlying cover. Don't laugh. We could be at golfing at home in New Jersey."

Matt called Harry, who was on patrol. Actually, he was sitting in his police car at Shelter Cove.

"Hi Harry, this is Matt," said Matt. "Are you busy?"

"Not at all, Matt," said Harry. "I'm just sitting on the side of the street waiting for something to happen. I go off duty in 15 minutes. What's up?"

"There is an abandoned part of Pease Air Force Base in New Hampshire that might be of interest to us. Do you know anything about it?"

"Not a thing, but Mary has relations there," answered Harry. "I'll give her a call and call you back"

Five minutes later, Harry called Matt.

"Here is the story," said Harry. "Pease has been off and on for years, and now it is a refueling base. It is extremely large. There are fuel tanks all over the place. There's an area of the property that has been given to conservation. So, do you want us to go up there and take a look?"

"Thanks for offering," said Matt. "Yes, and try to get back to me as soon as possible."

"This will be great," said Harry. "I owe Mary Brown a nice dinner for the lovable act we performed in the coffee shop to distract Joe, Atalus' watcher. There is an old restaurant in Kingston, New Hampshire named the 1686 House. She says it's pretty nice, and has tunnels in the basement to escape from Native Americans, years ago."

"Be sure to put that on your expenses," said Matt. "What's the deal with Joe, the follower?"

"Don't know," said Harry. "Haven't seen him after the first week. The boss must have felt it is okay. I did a check on Joe, and he is a big drinker, real time."

Okay, Harry," said Matt. "Let me know what's up there."

Matt left a message on Allen's cell phone, saying that they were looking into New Hampshire.

After the round of golf, Matt and the General headed for the 19th hole.

"Matt, are you getting tired of this project?" asked the General.

"No, not at all," said Matt. "For me, the more people involved, the better. We have to involve Clark's team though. I have a thought. We need to know what his Atalus' men are doing, and I think we can get it via the women in the bread store. What we can do is to station a couple of females from Clark's team in the bread store, and try to get a recording. Then we can get Allen Weinberg to translate it. I feel we have to hurry. It's just my intuition."

"Good idea," said the General. "I'll give Clark a buzz when we get back to the Big Dune."

Matt and the General headed back to the Big Dune. Allen Weinberg and Max Swift needed to look at a black box, and one was due this afternoon.

12

TO NEW HAMPSHIRE AND RETURN

"Should we fly or drive?" asked Mary.

"I thought about it," said Harry. "Let's drive. The government pays 25 cents per mile, and we can make a good profit. It's 1500 miles and it will take a little more than 15 hours."

"How long will that take us?" asked Mary "Did you say 15 hours? We'd better fly. Hold on a minute.

Mary accessed her cell phone. "$74 one way per person. Okay, thanks."

"We can rent a car, go to the site, and then go to the1686 House," said Mary. "I'll be ready in 15 minutes."

"Okay, I'll pick you up," said Harry, "Do you think they just have a plane waiting for us. We won't get a flight for a while."

"We'll work it out," replied Mary. "Should we wear our uniforms?"

"I think we should," said Harry. "We don't know what to expect."

The couple flew to Pease Air Force Base from Savannah Hilton Head Airport. There were no flights from Hilton Head. Harry was new to the southeast, and didn't even know that Hilton Head had two flight opportunities. There was one small airport on the island of Hilton Head, and one in Savannah. They rented a car at Pease and drove to the conservation site near the coast in Portsmouth. They surprised three men looking around the fuel tanks.

Harry looked at them and acted appropriately official.

"What are you guys doing here?" he asked, as he had his hand on the Police Special 38 on his side.

"We are just looking around, Sir," one of the men said. "We haven't touched anything."

"What are you looking for?" repeated Harry.

"We are only looking," said another of the men. "We would like to buy them."

"They are government property and contain fuel for airplanes," said Mary, and at that moment Harry stared at her, and she knew she had given too much information.

Harry talked to the three men for a while, acting as though they did nothing wrong.

The men were satisfied and went on their way.

Harry and Mary went on to the 1686 House in Kingston, New Hampshire. The dinner was luscious, and everything was as it was supposed to be. Afterwards, they headed back to Pease Air Base and arrived in Hilton Head before midnight. Not a word was spoken about the fuel tanks.

Harry had a good night's sleep and called Matt in the morning. Mary was standing next to him. He told Matt they were definitely middle-eastern and were looking at fuel tanks.

"Did you, by chance," asked Matt, "get a photo of them?"

"I didn't," said Harry. "I was too busy and didn't have any equipment for picture taking."

"I did," said Mary. "What do you thing I was doing while you were running your mouth off like you were their best friend."

"You have a good woman Harry," said Matt. "Mary's a star today."

"Anything new?" asked the General who was sitting next to Matt. "We've had a lot of action, and you seem to be in the middle of it."

"You're right. A lot is new," said Matt. "We know it's going to be avionic, even though we don't have the details. We have a photo of three of the suspects looking at fuel tanks in an unused part of Pease Air Force Base. The presumed leader Atalus is satisfied with the math tutor for his son. The watcher is no longer watching. I talked to Allen Weinberg, and he says as soon as they receive the next black box, we will be in good shape with the project. He asked about the ladies in the bread store talking Farsi without their Muslim hijabs. Maybe, Clark could put a team on this and Allen, while he is here, can make some sense of it."

"Okay, I'll do it," answered the General.

The last black box broke the bank, so to speak. The terrorist leader Atalus needed money badly. This got the General and Carter to move at a speed beyond belief. The Chinese connection was not responding to monetary requests and bills were adding up. General Clark decided to make a bold move. He had military intelligence sequester the young American lawyer and threatened to put him in prison for the rest of his life. All he had to do was to follow General Clark's orders, which were to deliver a large amount of money to Atalus and then disappear in the U.S. Government hierarchy. Clark provided the lawyer with $150,000 that the lawyer had to deliver to Atalus, and then leave the scene. The lawyer was not sure of how the money was sent to him and where it originated. The General and Clark wanted to run down the terrorists.

Clark's female team members Joyce Johnson and Michelle Hubinger were dispatched to the bread store to record the Muslim ladies without their knowledge. The Muslim ladies were worked up over the work of their husbands: three to New Hampshire and three to New Mexico. They were supposed to fly home to Hilton Head. The ladies changed their language from to English to Farsi, and the discussion moved on to the process of moving out of their apartments. In the ladies minds, things were in a total mess.

The ladies cut their coffee time shorter than usual, because they were all upset, and there was no pleasure in complaining. Joyce and Michelle were back in the Big Dune Hotel and Golf Courses in minutes. Allen was nervous and was in a hurry to hear the tape. Its contents were definitely worth the effort. The discussion of the Muslim ladies centered on the aircraft they would fly and how that would be arranged, and where they would go.. Their men seemed to have plenty of money and were also ordered to leave the United States. Also, they were disturbed about whether or not Atalus was leaving, as well. Finally, one of the Muslim women initiated a conversation on three seemingly unrelated places: the air control system in Cleveland, the air control system in Boston, and the air control system in Washington. For the ladies, their luxurious vacation in the United States was about to end.

Another subject on the black box was the talk to someone about auto pilots able to fly an aircraft without human intervention..

All of the information was relayed to Matt, and he just sat there piecing together the various items. Then he got a call.

"Hi, Matt," said Nancy Small. "I have news for you from the coffee shop. The tutoring is over. Apparently, the boy's teacher sent a message saying that tutoring was no longer needed. The boy was heart broken. He loved his tutor, since she was more like a mother to him. I am that person. He had a package for me from Atalus that contained $10,000 and a brief note. I'll read it to you:

> To Mrs. Nancy Small
> Thank you for taking care of my son.
> A small reward is enclosed.
> You are a remarkable woman.
> I would ask you to be my wife.
> I promise a glorious life for you.
> Atalus.

"Middle eastern men frequently have several wives," said Matt. "They usually have different purposes. The choice is yours. You can keep the money, but do not tell others about it. I'll see you in a general meeting later today."

"Are there other options available for me?" asked Nancy.

"I'll discuss it with the General and General Clark," said Matt. "There are always options."

<<<<<<<<<<<>>>>>>>>>>

"Sir, this is Matt," said Matt. "The tutoring over, and the kid liked Nancy Small. Atalus asked her to be his wife. Probably, she would actually be like the boy's nanny. Are there any options available to her from our view. Please check with Clark. I would like to advise her in our afternoon's Meeting."

The General talked to Clark, who read the General's mind before he was finished.

"I'll call the Director of Intelligence," said Clark. "I'll give you an immediate answer this afternoon. We have some experience with instances like this, and we know how to move quickly. I'll call her. Let's have lunch and I'll let you know."

<<<<<<<<<<<>>>>>>>>>>

Clark was a little late for lunch and the General figured it was because the DI was not immediately available. He had a smile on his face. The General knew it was good news from the standpoint of the United States.

"If she wants to be an intelligence source," said Clark, "We have an agent in Teheran who can run her in the field.

He can train her, and be a conduit for information. He will contact her in Iran. They use a communications signal and hers is *Practice Squad.* She will be right in the center of things."

"I'll let Matt know," replied the General. "Let's eat. The bill is on me."

PART III
THE RESULT

13

MATT MEETS WITH THE GENERALS

"There has been a lot of activity lately, so I thought I would bring you up to date on what's happened, and my analysis of it," said Matt. "I can support each and every judgment I have made."

"Sounds good, Matt," said the General. "I agree," said General Clark.

"First and foremost, this is a small job, and I think we have analyzed it thoroughly," said Matt. "Some organization would like to crash a plane into a Government building – probably the White House.. The sponsor is not necessarily from the same country as the active terrorists."

"Like who," said the General.

"Like the sponsor is China, and terrorists are Iranian," said Matt, "and the terrorists do not actually know who the sponsor is. The entity with the purse strings is an academic – dean or Professor – in Boston or possibly New

York Chinatown. The active shooter, to use the term loosely, is the Iranian. The process is clever. They will run aircrafts into Boston and Washington air traffic controllers, then an unidentified plane will crash into the White House. The small planes, like a small business jet, will hit Boston and Washington air traffic controllers and the larger plane, such as Gulfstream – a large model – will be heavily loaded with fuel and hit the target. By knocking out the controllers, our defense will be limited. The aircraft will be running on autopilot using artificial intelligence. The terrorists will be nowhere to be seen. We can know where the terrorist aircraft will be taking off from, using military radar. The planes will undoubtedly head out over the Atlantic Ocean and then head in to the continental United States. The first hit is in Boston, then the planes will progress to Washington, and then on to the target. That is the plan anyway. All we have to do is to set up a control post and command Air Force personnel to scramble F-35s to knockout the small aircraft with something like a sidewinder missile. The larger plane – loaded with fuel – will be trailed by the control center and the appropriate commander will scramble an F-22s to hit the enemy out over the Atlantic. The Pentagon will make a news release of defense testing and no one will be the wiser. The attack planes will not have pilots so we will not get into issues of killing people and items like that."

"What about the command center?" asked General Clark.

"Use a portable center like they use in combat operations," replied Matt.

"Where will it be located?" asked Clark.

"I suggest and recommend your residence in Sun City," said Matt. "We can bring in equipment under the guise of being HVAC equipment. It's small and can be removed in a few minutes. You undoubtedly have the capability to have that done."

"I do," said Clark. "Good planning Matt."

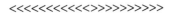

"Let's talk to Nancy Small," said General Clark to Matt and the General. "I want to get the other matter out of the way."

Matt handed Nancy a small slip of paper.

Here is what it said.

> *Nancy. If you want to go through with the operation, go to the ladies restroom. An associate will be waiting for you. You will be given a disguise. Go immediately to room 1538. You may be watched but probably not*

Nancy went to room 1538 and was met by Matt, the General, and General Clark.

"Nancy, you did remarkably will with the project," said the General. "If you want to go ahead with the Iran operation, you essentially have nothing to do. The Iranians will contact you and take you to Iran with them. You will probably be Atalus' nanny for the young fellow. Iranian men have wives for a purpose, such as nanny, housekeeper, computer scientist, and so forth. You will be a nanny and won't be a sex slave or anything like that. When you get there, you will be contacted by a controller and be advised about how you work to benefit the United States. Your security passcode is your protection. It is *Practice Squad.* We don't know who that is, but he or she will contact you. If life is unbearable, tell your controller. If things get serious, tell your controller, and we will extract you. We know how to do it, and the extraction will be handled by Matt, me, and perhaps even General Clark. The plane is a Gulfstream and the pilots will be former U.S. military pilots. Do not worry."

"We are setting up a government account for you and when you return, you will receive a signing bonus, annual salary, and a completion bonus," said General Clark. "If you need to be extracted, I will be there."

"If and when the Iranians have no need for you, they will send you home," said Matt. "We know more than you could ever guess. You will join the rest of the Iranians in a SWISS chartered plane. You will fly to Switzerland for refueling, and then on to Iran. We know this because the SWISS airline is an honest international partner and they have informed us. You will leave next Wednesday May 12th. That is, if you accept Mr. Atalus' offer. They will take care of everything. Ashley and I have had many Iranian students. They are trustworthy and honest people.

"You had better get back to the ladies rest room. Good luck and god speed."

Nancy gave each of the men a hug and left.

<<<<<<<<<<<<<>>>>>>>>>>>

"Thanks, gentlemen," said Matt. "I'm optimistic that things will work out as planned."

"I hope you are right," said General Clark.

That evening, Nancy accepted the offer made by Atalus.

14

THE AIRCRAFT AND THE CONTROL CENTER

The three terrorists landed in New Mexico and took a taxi to the airplane storage facility where thousands of used aircraft are stored for whatever reason. It was a quiet weekend and the product manager was lounging in his office. It was his turn to run the facility on a weekend day. Nothing had ever happened on a Saturday or Sunday.

The Iranian terrorist individuals spoke perfect English and convinced the manager that they could fly and showed their pilot's license with instrument rating. They said they wanted to buy several airplanes. First the three unknown terrorists looked at a couple of Lear Jets that looked in perfect condition. The manager said he could never sell them as private business jets were almost always purchased new. The written agreement was prepared and the manager asked for their passports. He was totally surprised that all had a U.S. passport and South Carolina driver's license. He asked if they had money or did they want to finance their purchase. One of the Iranians said, "Cash." The manager said, "What kind of cash? Currency, checks, or credit card."

The Iranian agreed to pay currency, for which the manager added a 10% stipend for himself.

One of the Iranians said," One more."

"What would you like?" said the manager.

"Gulfstream with easy entry for luggage," said the Iranian. "Maybe Gulfstream 650."

"Are you sure you want such a large airplane?" asked the Manager.

"That one over there," said the Iranian pointing to a seemingly worn out Gulfstream 650.

"I'll give you a good price, and add fuel for all three airplanes," said the Manager.

The Iranians negotiated a good price for the Gulfstream and in an hour, the three planes were headed east. The Iranians flew the airplanes straight through to New Hampshire, stopping for fuel and food only when necessary. They landed after dawn at the abandoned area of Pease Air Force Base.

The minute the three planes landed in New Hampshire, an electrical engineer, an aeronautical engineer, and an aircraft technician started to modify the planes to fly under a new form of autopilot. All they needed was take off capability, and the ability to fly under computer control using artificial intelligence.

The men went to a hotel in Portsmouth, New Hampshire and slept for 16 hours. One of them called Atalus, and he gave him instructions for the major operations that were to begin at 6:00 am on Wednesday.

Atalus' man Joe that performs just about anything necessary brought the team money and the plan for meeting their families and leaving the country.

The terrorist operation had effectively been initiated. They were going to have the planes they purchased modified and then crashed into three locations. That is the way with terrorists. They would never even learn who was the sponsor.

General Clark ordered the Army Combat Engineering Group to install a long-range combat control center in his villa in Sun City. He even had a modern radar tower that looked like a TV antenna, all delivered in a HVAC truck. Clark was talking to the guy across the street, who was one of those people that needed to be the first person in the neighborhood to meet the newcomers. In this case, he and his wife had purchased an inexpensive residence and poured an enormous amount of cash into it. Most people thought he was hiding something from the tax people. In fact, any time something happened and the authorities were involved, he was right there listening.

Clark's installation was complete and a young fellow approached General Clark and said, "We've finished the job, Sir."

You could practically hear the neighbor's eyeballs click. General Clark, who was not known by his professional affiliation, became a person of interest.

At this point, things were ready to go by the terrorists, but when? Matt contacted Harry and asked him to go up to Pease Air Force Base in New Hampshire to scout things out. Harry was a licensed pilot, and the General agreed to let him fly Little Man up to Pease.

Harry and Mary landed at Pease, rented a car, and headed to Portsmouth.

Harry and Mary were dressed as hikers and wandered about the conservation site being used by the terrorists.

"Matt, they are ready to go," said Harry. "The planes are loaded with fuel, and the men are hunkered down in a small trailer. I'd say that they will go at first light tomorrow."

Matt was talking to the General when Harry's call came in.

"I think tomorrow is the day, General," said Matt. "Will you inform General Clark?"

"Will do," said the General.

The General called Clark and gave him the news. Clark had enlisted men to man the radar continuously. The guess was that the operation would begin tomorrow about 6 am.

"I'm assuming that the operation will take place as planned," said the General. "How did you ever figure it out? You saved very many people's lives and Government property."

"You know me, Sir," answered Matt. "I just ran through all of the possibilities, and that was the only scenario that matched the data."

"Well, it's out of our hands,: said the General. "Thank you for what you have done."

15

THE ATTACK

The sun rose at Pease Air Force Base at approximately 6:00 am. The terrorists were out of their trailer, and the leader accessed the control computer. The autopilots in the planes were programmed differently: the first for the Boston Air Control Center, the second for the Washington Air Control Center, and the third was for the White House. The flight paths for all three were out over the Atlantic Ocean and back in to the targets in the United States.

At the same time, the three fighter control defense groups were ready.

When the first terrorist plane, headed for the Boston Air Control Center lifted off, two F-35s took off at high speed from the New Hampshire defense base. They had one and only one objective. Ask their target for identification, and if none was returned, they were instructed to fire sidewinder missiles and destroy the terrorist plane completely. In 10 minutes, it was done. A large ball of fire was all that was left.

Two minutes after the first, the second terrorist plane, headed for the Washington Air Control Center lifted off. Immediately, two F-35s took off at high speed from the Washington defense base. The second terrorist plane was asked for identification. None was returned so sidewinders from the fighters destroyed the second terrorist plane completely. A second ball of fire was all that was left of the terrorist plane.

The terrorists at this point thought that both the Boston and Washington Centers would be done and the Gulfstream 650 loaded with fuel had a clear shot at the White House. Nothing could be farther from the truth. It was fired from the terrorist base out into the Atlantic Ocean and turned around to face two F-22 Raptors. Identification was requested, and none was returned, since all of the terrorist planes were traveling under artificial intelligence controlled autopilot. The Raptors fired their high yield defense missiles at the terrorist Gulfstream 650 and it was destroyed completely. Three large balls of fire could now be scene from a distance. The fighter planes returned to their bases. It was all in a day's work for the pilots.

The Department of Defense news bureau released a short memo stating that there had been some testing in the Atlantic Ocean, just off the coast.

General Clark at his home at 404 Rolling Hills Lane in Sun City said, "Targets destroyed. Time to shut down. You will all receive a combat medal of honor. The event you witnessed is classified at the highest level. Thank you."

16

THE FLIGHT HOME

The General's team, at least the Boston and New Jersey people, were headed to Boston to drop off Allen Weinberg and his wife. The General had ordered a limousine to transport them to their home.

"You will receive the complete honorarium of $200,000.00," said the General to Dr. Weinberg. "It will deposited in one week to the bank account number you gave to Matt. You have been an immeasurable asset to our team. Thank you very much."

The plane left Boston and headed for New Jersey. Matt put the jet on autopilot at 300 mph at 30,000 feet. He leaned back and stretched.

"I would have liked to see that home in Sun City," said Matt. "It is the perfect location for a golfer. Sun City has three courses."

"You will," said the General. "I have purchased the villa at 508 Rolling Hills Lane. It's in your name, and Ashley is the second owner in case something happens to the primary owner. Thank you for your hard work and keen intellect."

"Thank you, Sir," said Matt. "This is unbelievable."

"It had 3 bedrooms and a golf room and all of the other rooms," said the General.

"Oh, we left our clubs at the Big Dune," said Matt.

"You haven't," said the General. "They have already been transferred to your new home. By the way, we should expect a trip to the White House. The President is pleased with our work."

"Do we have furniture for the home in Sun City?" asked Matt.

"I will ask Ashley and Anna to do that during our next trip."

The rest of the trip ended smoothly and everyone was cheerful. Even the course at the New Jersey Country Club seemed good.

17

THE WHITE HOUSE

The President did invite the team to the White House, without a stated agenda.

Everyone joined in a White House dinner, and afterwards the President made an announcement.

"Ladies and Gentlemen," said the President. "I have some awards to present. General Clark you are hereby awarded your fifth star. Congratulations. Matthew Miller, General Les Miller, Ashley Miller, and Marguerite Pourgoine will be awarded the National Medal of Freedom. Ashley, this is your second award. Thank you."

"And one more thing," as the honorable Steve Jobs used to say. "General Miller, you have already been awarded an additional star. You are hereby awarded a Medal of Achievement to be worn on your dress uniform. Thank you all."

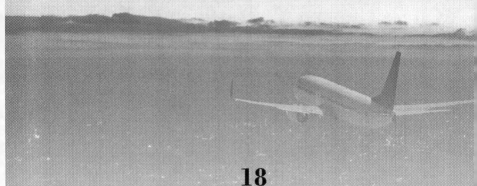

18

BACK IN NEW JERSEY

On the first free Saturday, Matt and the General were back on the golf course at the Country Club. The weather was exceptionally good and all of the pressure was off. As usual, Matt initiated a conversation after the 9th hole.

"The course seems as though it is back to normal," said Matt. "It's possible I was wrong when I said the course looked shabby."

"I agree," replied the General. "I guess we were both wrong, but we made some money and helped the country when it needed our help."

"And got a medal," said Matt.

"What did you do with yours?" asked the General.

"I gave it to my Mom," said Matt. "She's interested in things like that."

"What did Ashley do with her second medal?" asked the General.

"She gave it to her mother," said Matt. "The easiest solution is the best one."

"When is your next trip to Sun City?" asked the General.

"Next week," said Matt. "We are both off for a week. You're invited. I would like to try the newest course called Argent Lakes at Sun City."

"Thank you," said the General. "Anna will enjoy the trip. Are you free for dinner at the Green Room tonight?"

"We are," said Matt. "We'll be there at 6:00."

19

THE AFTERWARD

In an adventure like this, most people would like to know what happened to the characters,

To everyone's surprise, the house on Folding Island Road in Hilton Head was vacated by the leader when the terrorists left the country. There was a clause in the sales contract that if the property were vacated, the ownership of the property would revert back to the former owner. The former owner was a lawyer by trade before he retired, and he set it up that way. No one noticed it when the contract was signed.

Matt and Ashley spend some of their free time in Sun City and enjoy the extensive facilities offered by that gated development.

The General and Anna spent a lot of time in Klosters in Switzerland along with Sir Charles Bunday and his wife.

But the following is the most exciting episode of them all.

What ever happened to Nancy Small, the tutor that accepted a position as the wife of Atalus, the Iranian terrorist leader?

Nancy became an academic nanny for Atalus' son. She connected well with her controller and learned how to be a spy in a foreign country. The White House attack that failed was written off as an operational failure. The next major event was expected to be to crash a plane into Buckingham Palace in London. Nancy learned of it through her work as a nanny and turned the expected event over to her controllers. Again, the second attack was a failure and an investigation of what went wrong was initiated. The only common denominator was Nancy, the nanny. Atalus and his team were moved and Nancy, the ex Nanny, was left alone. With no roots, she was afraid. Then on the morning of the day before a Muslim holy day, her controller advised her that her cover was blown, and both of them had to be extracted from Iran. The controller advised her contacts in the States of the situation

There is a landing strip in the southeast corner of Iran built for Russian Sukhoi SU-57 fighter planes. It was built for SU-57s and then the order did not materialize and the base was left vacant. That is where the pickup would be made.

He extraction would involve two similar automobiles: armor plated Mercedes S500 sedans of the same color. They had reliable drivers paid by the U.S. government, and were generally available. Each extracted person rode in a separate car for security reasons. They would leave early on the holy day as everything was shut down. They would be picked up at noon on the strip at Sukhoi field. There would be two escape aircraft. For Nancey, Matt and the General plus General Mark Clark had committed to extract her in the event she needed to be removed because her cover was blown.

Back in the States, Matt and the General had planned a day of golf followed by a dinner at the Green Room. They had to do the extraction, and the process had been planned. The General's Gulfstream was in Langley. The extraction event went through military channels and a fast jet was sent to New Jersey to pick them up. They would fly to Langley and then take the Gulfstream to the Sukhoi base. On the way home, the Gulfstream would stop at Goose Bay for refueling.

The General requested an escort through Iranian airspace and an F-117A stealth fighter was assigned to the task from an aircraft carrier. The F-117A was invisible to radar and was fully equipped with armament and new electronics that could disable an enemy's electronics. When the Gulfstream entered Iranian airspace, it would be escorted by the F-117A through an aircraft corridor.

Matt and the General put on military fatigues and started the trip to Iran.

The Gulfstream 650 had three pilots, as it was a very long flight. The Gulfstream stopped at Goose Bay for refueling and then continued on to Iran. As the Gulfstream 650 entered Iranian airspace, the F-117A picked them up. The F-117A was invisible to radar, but the Gulfstream was not. The Gulfstream 650 was detected by Iranian radar, and a MIG 35 fighter was scrambled to check it out. The F-117A had a choice to destroy the MIG-35 or simply disable its electronics requiring it to limp back to home base. A decision was made to avoid an international incident, so it simply disabled the electronics in the MIG-35.

Matt and the General plus General Mark Carter picked up Nancy and proceeded to the States as planned. The return flight landed at Langley and then the passengers were delivered – except for Clark – by fast jet to New Jersey. The next day the General arranged a meeting of Nancy and her husband. He had finally made it to first team and then suffered an ACL injury. They met in the Marriott Hotel in Copley Plaza and had an enjoyable dinner at Legal Seafood's. Nancy explained that she was an academic nanny and nothing more. Things went well and Nancy received a Medal of Honor, and the couple is doing well in upstate New Hampshire.

Now, that's the real end of the story. Thank you for reading it.

ABOUT THE BOOK

This book is a novel that was written solely for entertainment. The characters, places and events are all the product of the author's imagination. Of course, events and places with the same name, do in fact, exist but not necessarily in the manner given. Those entities are created to serve the plot of the story. For example, an Iranian air base named Sukhoi is purely fictitious.

Most of the included information on airplanes and related phenomena are essentially true, but possibly out of date in some cases.

The team consisting of Matt, the General, Ashley, and Anna does not exist in real life, except by an extreme coincidence.

The flights of the General's Gulfstream 650 are a bit exaggerated but could actually happen. The manner in which money is disbursed is not at all true and used for entertainment.

In summary, the book is a made-up collection of people and events that aren't true, and the conclusion hasn't happened. But you never know, it could end up being true.

The author would like to thank his wife Margaret for helping with the manuscript.

This book adheres to the author's policy of no sex, no violence, and no bad language.

ABOUT THE AUTHOR

Harry Katzan, Jr. is a professor who has written books and papers on computer science and service science, in addition to few novels, and has been a consultant to the executive board of a major bank. He and his wife have lived in Switzerland where he was a consultant and a visiting professor. He holds bachelors, masters, and doctorate degrees.

Printed in the United States
by Baker & Taylor Publisher Services